Friends to the Rescue

by

SCOTT HIGGS

Scholastic Canada Ltd.

Toronto New York London Auckland Sydney
Mexico City New Delhi Hong Kong Buenos Aires

For Alexa
— S.H.

The illustrations in this book were inked by hand,
then scanned, coloured and shaded in Photoshop.

The text type was set in 20 pt Maiandra GD.

Scholastic Canada Ltd.
604 King Street West, Toronto, Ontario M5V 1E1, Canada

Scholastic Inc.
557 Broadway, New York, NY 10012, USA

Scholastic Australia Pty Limited
PO Box 579, Gosford, NSW 2250, Australia

Scholastic New Zealand Limited
Private Bag 94407, Greenmount, Auckland, New Zealand

Scholastic Children's Books
Euston House, 24 Eversholt Street, London NW1 1DB, UK

Library and Archives Canada Cataloguing in Publication
Higgs, Scott
Friends to the rescue / Scott Higgs, author and illustrator.
(Haley & Bix)
ISBN-13: 978-0-439-93765-8
ISBN-10: 0-439-93765-5

I. Title. II. Series: Higgs, Scott. Haley and Bix.
PS8615.I38F75 2007 jC813'.6 C2006-904658-1

6 5 4 3 2 1 Printed in Canada 07 08 09 10 11

Even though Haley and Bix were very different, there was no doubt about it.

They were best friends.

They played together every single day.
Sometimes Bix chose the game.

Sometimes Haley did.

No matter who chose, both girls always had fun.

But one day Bix didn't feel like playing.

Haley was surprised. “What on earth is wrong, Bix?”

“Haley, this is no time for playing games! Endangered animals all over the world need our help!”

"Don't you worry, Bix, we will save those animals!"

Haley got busy. She and Bix would need plenty of equipment.

Bix got straight to work on
special outfits.

The girls loaded up Bix's wagon and set out to find animals in danger.

They did not have to go very far.

Frisco was the neighbours' cat.
He was on top of a very narrow fence.

"Haley, Frisco isn't safe. He could fall. I think he is endangered."

"You're right, Bix. We have to help him!"

The girls carefully loaded Frisco into Bix's wagon.
"Now you are saved, Frisco."

At first Frisco wouldn't stay saved.

But Haley found some beef jerky in her pocket, and that did the trick.

At the very next house, the girls saw Mrs. Parker's dog, Bailey.

"Oh my gosh! Bailey is tied to a tree! He's going to choke for sure!"

Haley and Bix saved Bailey.

Snowball and Oreo lived in the yard next to Bailey's.

Haley didn't like the looks of their hutch. "That seems very drafty to me. Those bunnies will catch a chill."

It turned out even bunnies could be endangered.

The girls found animals to save all over the neighbourhood.

They were surprised at how many could fit into Bix's wagon.

But not as surprised as Bix's father.

Bix's mother explained. "These pets are not endangered. Endangered animals live in the wild."

Haley and Bix thought for a moment.
They still wanted to help.
"Let's raise money to save the wild animals!"

Bix suggested a bake sale.

“We can sell cream puffs and ladyfingers!”

Haley thought a rodeo or a demolition derby would be more fun.

Then Bix had an idea.
They would have a pet wash.

It was a very good idea . . .

because even though none of
the neighbourhood pets needed
to be saved,

quite a few of them needed baths.

All afternoon the girls splashed and scrubbed, cuddled and combed.

By the end of the day, the pets were happy to be clean. The neighbours were happy to have their pets back.

And Haley and Bix were happy to have helped.